LAUREL VALLEY STORE

Epossumondas Saves the Day

WRITTEN BY **Coleen Salley**

ILLUSTRATED BY **Janet Stevens**

Harcourt, Inc.
Orlando   Austin   New York
San Diego   Toronto   London

Library of Congress Cataloging-in-Publication Data
Salley, Coleen.
Epossumondas saves the day/written by Coleen Salley;
illustrated by Janet Stevens.
p.   cm.
Summary: In this variation on the folktale Sody Sallyraytus, each of Epossumondas's
birthday guests disappears until it is finally up to him to rescue them all and bring
home the "sody" for his birthday biscuits.
[1. Missing persons—Fiction.   2. Opossums—Fiction.   3. Snapping turtles—Fiction.
4. Turtles—Fiction.   5. Birthdays—Fiction.   6. Louisiana—Fiction.]   I. Stevens, Janet, ill.
II. Title.
PZ7.S15327Epo 2006
[E]—dc22   2005027538
ISBN-13: 978-0-15-205701-5
ISBN-10: 0-15-205701-3

First edition
H G F E D C B A

Manufactured in China

The illustrations in this book were done in mixed media
on watercolor paper.
The display type was set in Pumpkin JF.
The text type was set in Big Dog.
Color separations by Bright Arts Ltd., Hong Kong
Manufactured by South China Printing Company, Ltd., China
This book was printed on totally chlorine-free
Stora Enso Matte paper.
Production supervision by Jane Van Gelder
Designed by Lydia D'moch

For my dear friend Janet Stevens, who
immortalized me in her art, and for my
brilliant young editor, Jeannette Larson,
who gently brings out the best in her
authors and illustrators
—C. S.

For Ted, who has supported me through
all the ups and downs of bookmaking
—J. S.

Thanks to my milliner, Riva Stover, who makes
the hats that delight my audiences—C. S.

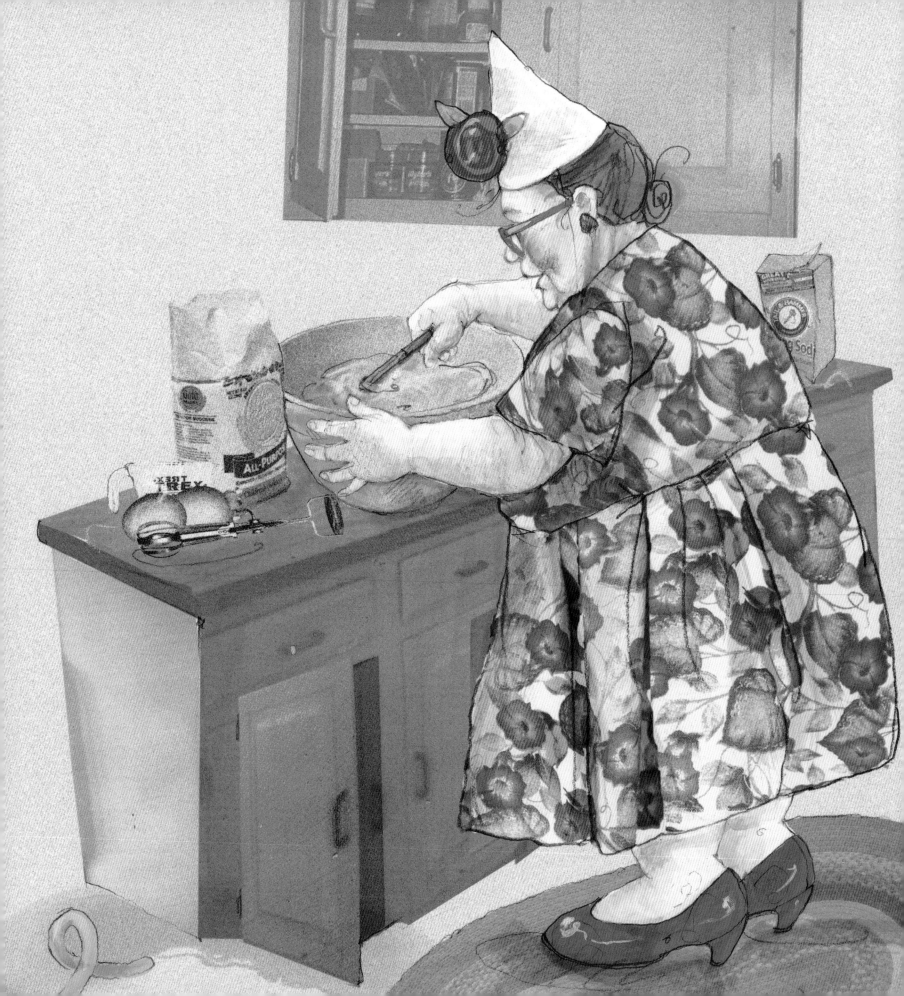

Once upon a time, but maybe not so long ago, Epossumondas and his mama lived in a little cottage back by the sugarcane fields in Laurel Valley on Bayou Lafourche. Auntie lived down the road a piece.

It was Epossumondas's birthday, and he and Mama were getting ready for his party. Epossumondas was squeezing lemons for the lemonade. Mama was making his favorite dessert: strawberry shortcake—not the kind made with cake, but the kind made with sweet biscuits. She put all the mixings in her big bowl and reached for her sody sallyraytus. The box was empty! And you know you can't make big, light, fluffy biscuits without sody sallyraytus.

"Well, I swaney!" cried Mama. "This is what happens when you wait till the last minute."

"Can I go get the sody for you, please?" Epossumondas said.

"No, sweetie, I need your help with the lemonade, so you keep on squeezing. I'll go myself."

Just then, Baby Gator arrived early for the party.
"Oh, good!" Mama cried. "Honey, could you scoot over
to the store and get me a box of sody sallyraytus? Tell
Mr. Leslie to put it on my bill and come on back here
lickety-split. Don't dillydally!"

So Baby Gator skipped along the creek that meanders catawampus through the fields, singing, "Sody! Sody! Sody sallyraytus!" He crossed the creek, jumping on the stepping-stones—one, two, three—and then ran into the store and asked for the sody.

He thanked Mr. Leslie and skipped out, singing, "Sody! Sody! Sody sallyraytus!"

But when he got back to the creek . . .

... the biggest stepping-stone moved and a head rared up out of it! It wasn't a stone at all! It was a **GREAT, HUGE, UGLY LOUISIANA SNAPPING TURTLE!** That snapper snarled, "Baby Gator, you woke me up. I'm hungry, and I'm gonna eat you and your sody sallyraytus." And he swallowed Baby Gator and his sody in one big gulp!

Well, back home, Mama was about to have a hissy fit because Baby Gator was nowhere in sight.

"I've been squeezing and squeezing, Mama," Epossumondas said. "Can I go get the sody for you, please?"

"No, honey, I need you to set up that pin-the-tail game. I'll go myself."

Just then, Auntie arrived. "Oh, thank goodness!" Mama said. "Sister, will you go down to the store and see if you can find that poky Baby Gator with my sody sallyraytus?"

Auntie galumphed along toward Bayou Lafourche, mumbling, "Sody! Sody! Sody sallyraytus!" She crossed the stepping-stones—one, two, three—and galumphed into the store.

Mr. Leslie said, "Why, that little rascal left a long time ago. He must be dawdling in the creek. Here's another box of sody just in case."

So Auntie galumphed back, mumbling, "Sody! Sody! Sody sallyraytus!" But when she got to the creek . . .

...that GREAT, HUGE, UGLY LOUISIANA SNAPPING TURTLE rared up and growled, "Old auntie, I just ate a baby gator and his sody sallyraytus. Now I'm gonna eat you, too." And he swallowed Auntie and her sody in one big gulp!

Back at the house, Mama was soppin' mad. "Where did they get to? They could go to Plum Nelly and back in this much time!"

"The pin-the-tail is ready, Mama," Epossumondas said. "Can I go get the sody for you, please?"

"No, sugar pie, I need your help with the balloons. There's hanging to be done. I'll go myself."

Mama stomped off, grumbling, "Sody! Sody! Sody sallyraytus!" She stomped over the stepping-stones—one, two, three—and went into the store.

"Land sakes!" said Mr. Leslie. "They wouldn't BOTH be dawdling in the creek. I can't imagine where they are. Here, you'd better take two boxes of sody just in case."

So Mama stomped back toward the creek, grumbling, "Sody! Sody! Sody sallyraytus!" But when she got there, you know what happened, don't you?

That GREAT, HUGE, UGLY LOUISIANA
SNAPPING TURTLE rared up and growled,
"Old mama, I just ate a baby gator and his
sody, and an old auntie and her sody—she
looked a lot like you, come to think of it. Now
I'm gonna eat you, too." And he swallowed
Mama and her sody in one big gulp!

Back at home, Epossumondas was wondering what was keeping everyone. He'd been hanging and hanging and STILL no one came home. That little possum was getting as nervous as a long-tailed cat in a roomful of rocking chairs.

"What happened to everyone?"
Epossumondas said to himself. "No Baby
Gator, no Auntie, no Mama—no party!
I'd better go find them myself!"

So Epossumondas skedaddled along the road, shouting, "Sody! Sody! Sody sallyraytus!" He ran across the stepping-stones—one, two, three—and skedaddled right into the store.

When Mr. Leslie saw him, that man was flabbergasted! "Good gracious! I don't know where all your folks are! You'd better take all the sody just in case."

So Epossumondas started back, shouting, "Sody! Sody! Sody sallyraytus!" But when he got to the creek . . .

. . . that GREAT, HUGE, UGLY LOUISIANA SNAPPING
TURTLE rared up and stuck out his scrawny, wrinkled
neck. "GRRR!"

"Thumpin' gizzards!" gasped Epossumondas.
"I thought you were a stepping-stone—but you're
a GREAT, HUGE, UGLY LOUISIANA SNAPPING TURTLE!"

"You're right, possum—I am a GREAT, HUGE, UGLY
LOUISIANA SNAPPING TURTLE. And I'm hungry. I just
ate an old mama and her sody, an old auntie and her
sody, and a baby gator and his sody!"

"Mr. Snapper, you couldn't have eaten all of them!
That's just too mean!"

"Possum, my whole self is just filled up with mean juice. So now I'm gonna eat you, too!"

The old turtle snapped at Epossumondas. But just before his jaws clamped down, that little possum hollered, "Don't eat me! It's my birthday, and I haven't even had my party yet!" He hightailed it up the nearest cypress tree, screaming his head off all the way.

That GREAT, HUGE, UGLY LOUISIANA SNAPPING TURTLE wasn't going to let Epossumondas get away so fast. He lumbered up to that tree and growled all the louder, opening his humongous jaws wide.

Epossumondas hollered, "Mr. Snapper, you'd better spit out my folks or you'll be sorry!"

"Huh! What can a puny little critter like you do to me?" And then that old turtle started bumping his head so hard against the cypress tree Epossumondas thought he might tumble right out.

He squeezed his eyes shut and threw the only thing he had: a box of sody sallyraytus! GULP! That sody went right down the turtle's throat. Then he threw a second box—GULP! And another and another—GULP! GULP!

Now you may not know this, but when that much sody mixes with all the mean juice inside a GREAT, HUGE, UGLY LOUISIANA SNAPPING TURTLE, something unbelievable happens. That ornery old snapper puffed up like a big, light, fluffy biscuit. Epossumondas held tight to his branch and kept his eyes squeezed shut. The GREAT, HUGE, UGLY LOUISIANA SNAPPING TURTLE got bigger and bigger and rounder and rounder and then floated right off the ground, higher and higher until—

POP!

He burst wide open just like a birthday
balloon. Out tumbled . . .

MAMA,

and

BABY GATOR

...all in perfect shape.

AUNTIE,

"Oh, my sweet little patootie saved us! Honey, you're gooder 'n' grits," cried Mama. "And look at this—one box of sody sallyraytus was safe in my purse. Now we can make some biscuits for our little hero!"

So everyone marched home, singing, "Sody! Sody! Sody sallyraytus!"

And then they had the best birthday party
for the bravest possum ever:

EPOSSUMONDAS!

A Note from the Author

SODY SALLYRAYTUS is an old Southern term for "baking soda."
Variations on this story about sody have been told in the South
for generations.

Laurel Valley is a real place, first settled in 1785. Located
on the banks of Bayou Lafourche in southern Louisiana, it is
America's largest surviving sugar plantation. Many of its
original slave and tenant houses, built in the nineteenth century,
have been preserved. Some have been fully restored by the non-
profit organization Friends of Laurel Valley Village with the help
of the citizens of Thibodaux, the National Park Service, and
the Louisiana Department of Labor. Dr. J. Paul Leslie, professor of
history at Nicholls State University, was a major organizer of the
project and worked alongside disadvantaged teenagers who joined
the restoration to gain practical career skills. Laurel Valley Village
celebrates its heritage at festivals each spring and fall.

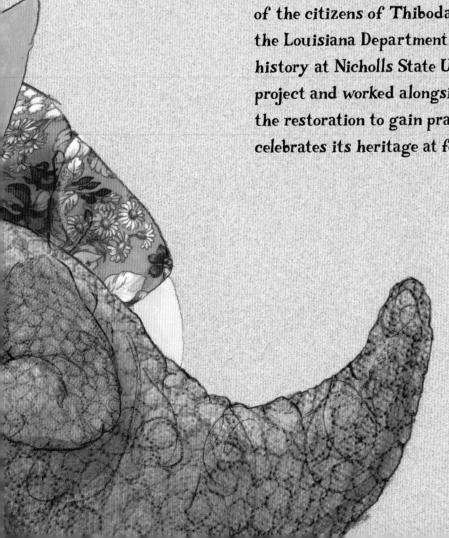